Crunchy, Not Sweet

by Amy Ward

KWiL Publishing

Hoppity'

ploppity...

...Little Tree Dude.

Clinging and swinging...

...and thinkin' bout food.

Dude's diet is boring.
It's time for exploring.

He's in a hungry,
try-anything mood.

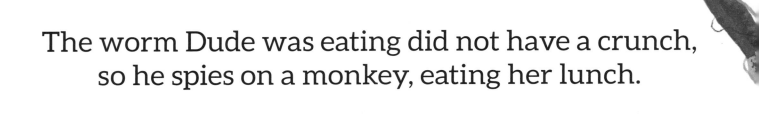

The worm Dude was eating did not have a crunch,
so he spies on a monkey, eating her lunch.

He takes a big bite…

...but something's not right!

Too mushy!

Too sweet!

And there's no crunch to munch!

Dude hears some loud birds snip-snacking away...
...on berries with seeds; he joins their buffet.

He plucks one to eat …

...but it's terribly sweet!

He's starting to think maybe worms are okay.

(But worms are so boring!
He needs more exploring!)

Dude checks out a squirrel devouring a nut.
This crunch is as noisy as Dude's empty gut!

But Dude cannot hack it!
There's no way to crack it.

And that puts
this frog in a
deep
no-food
rut!

Zip-zipping and flipping, a dark spot zooms by.

The sound is appealing. He thinks he knows why!

Dude looks all about.

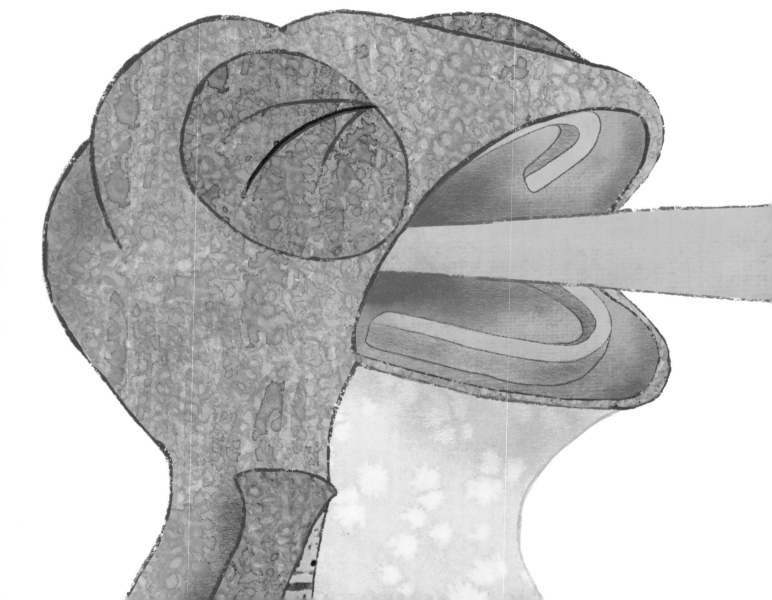

His tongue lashes out!

He snaps it! He slurps it!

What is it?

A fly!

Hooray for exploring!
This fly isn't boring.

It's crunchy, not sweet…

The perfect frog treat.

Frog Facts:

Dude is a red-eyed tree frog.

Red-eyed tree frogs are carnivores.

Carnivores eat meat, not plants.

Dude's diet does not include bananas, berries, or nuts.

It does include worms and insects, like flies!

For all my boys:
Pat, Jackson, Max, and Cade
~Amy

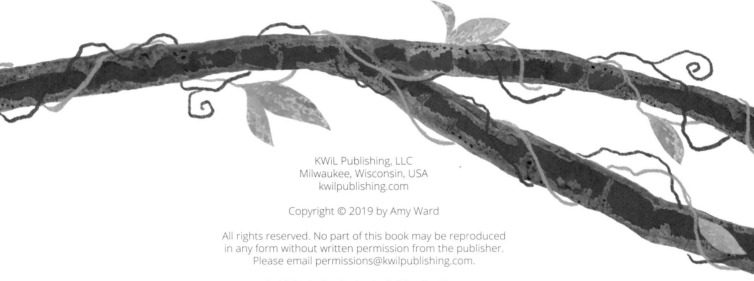

KWiL Publishing, LLC
Milwaukee, Wisconsin, USA
kwilpublishing.com

Publisher's Cataloging-in-Publication Data

Names: Ward, Amy, author.
Title: Crunchy, not sweet / by Amy Ward.
Description: Milwaukee, WI: KWiL Publishing, LLC, 2019.
Identifiers: ISBN 978-0-9991437-2-8 | LCCN 2018945386
Summary: A tree frog searches for a snack that is crunchy but not sweet.
Subjects: LCSH Tree frogs—Juvenile fiction. | Food—Juvenile fiction.
Nature—Juvenile fiction. | Picture Books for Children.
BISAC JUVENILE FICTION / Animals / Reptiles & Amphibians
Classification: LCC PZ7 .W1855 Cr 2019 | DDC [E]—dc23

The illustrations in this book were created with watercolor
and crayon resist and digital collaging techniques.
Text set in Aleo. Display type is Meatloaf Solid.
Book design by Sheri Roloff.

Printed at Worzalla in Stevens Point, Wisconsin, USA

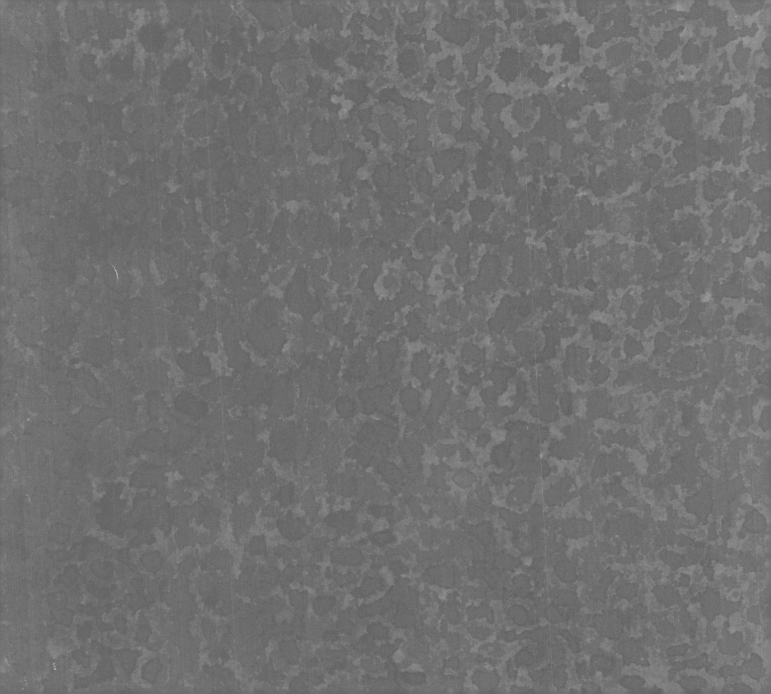